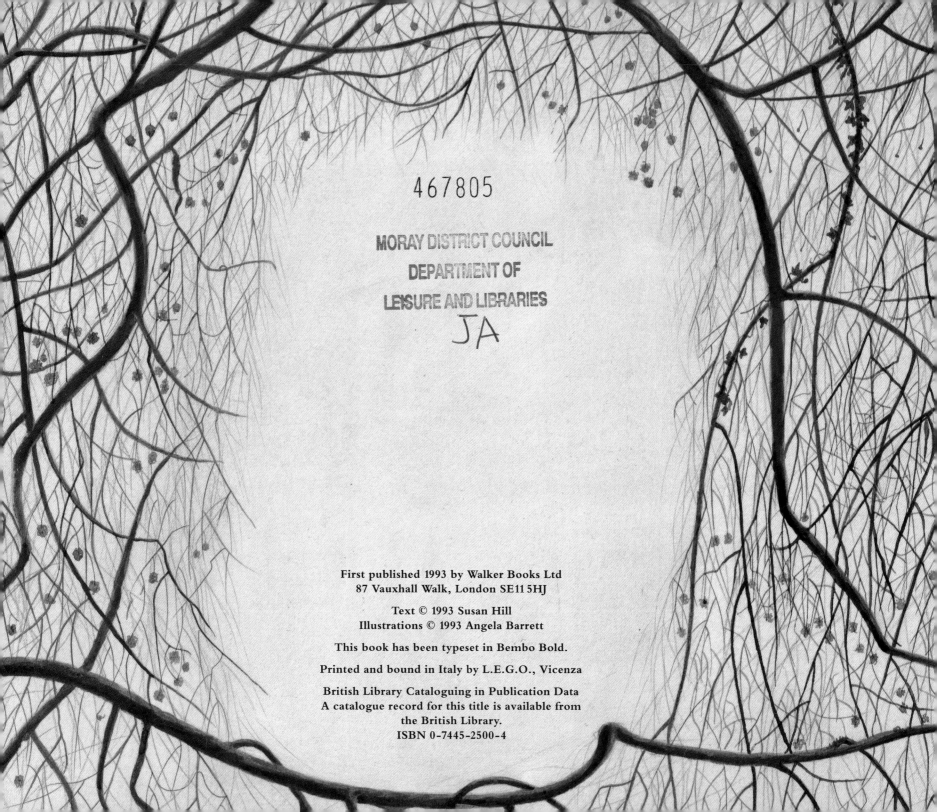

First published 1993 by Walker Books Ltd
87 Vauxhall Walk, London SE11 5HJ

Text © 1993 Susan Hill
Illustrations © 1993 Angela Barrett

This book has been typeset in Bembo Bold.

Printed and bound in Italy by L.E.G.O., Vicenza

British Library Cataloguing in Publication Data
A catalogue record for this title is available from
the British Library.
ISBN 0-7445-2500-4

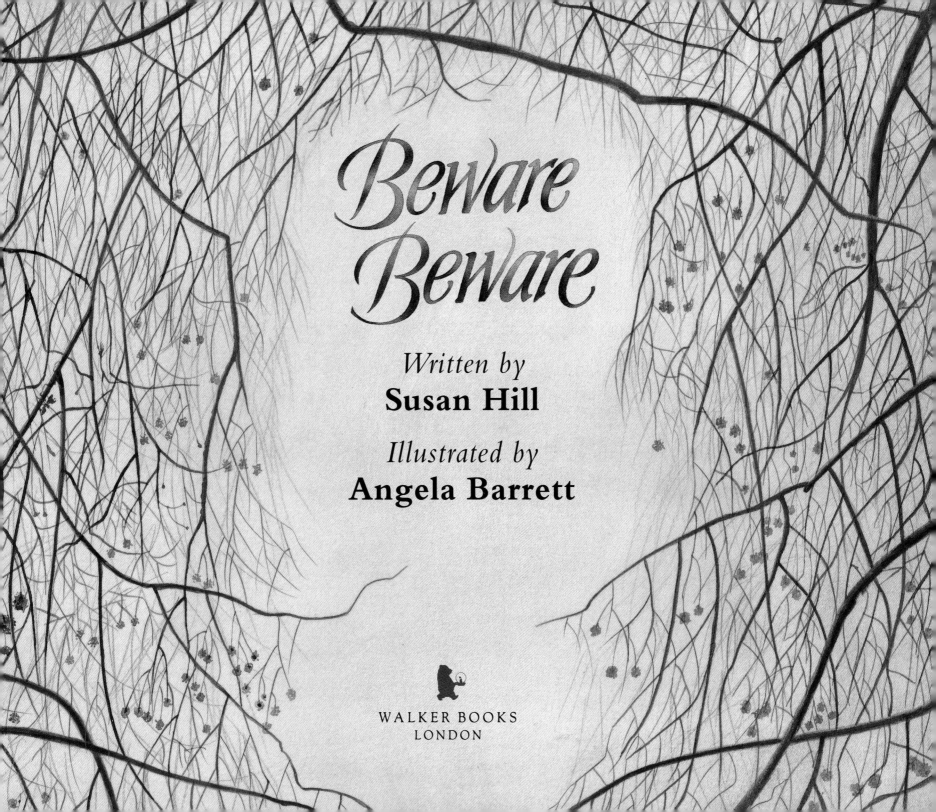

Beware Beware

Written by
Susan Hill

Illustrated by
Angela Barrett

WALKER BOOKS
LONDON

Kitchen's warm.

Smells of spice.

Kettle sings.

Fire bright.

But what's out there?

Beware, beware.

Setting sun

Rose red.

Light falls

Across the snow.

Path winds.

Who's to know?

Don't go!

But what's out there?

Slip down

Softly creep

Lift the latch

Snow's deep

In long shadow lies the wood.

I knew I could!

I'm here, out there.

Beware, beware!

I will take care.

Birds cold

Branches bare

What's over there?

Not far.

I can look back

I'm taking care

I'm there! I'm there!

Twig cracks

Dead leaves

No snow in the wood

Quiet. Safe. Dry.

Good.

What's there? What's there?

Beware! Beware!

Trolls Goblins

Elves Sprites

Mysterious lights

Fingers beckon

Eyes stare

Wolf

Bear

Dragon's lair

Beware! Beware!

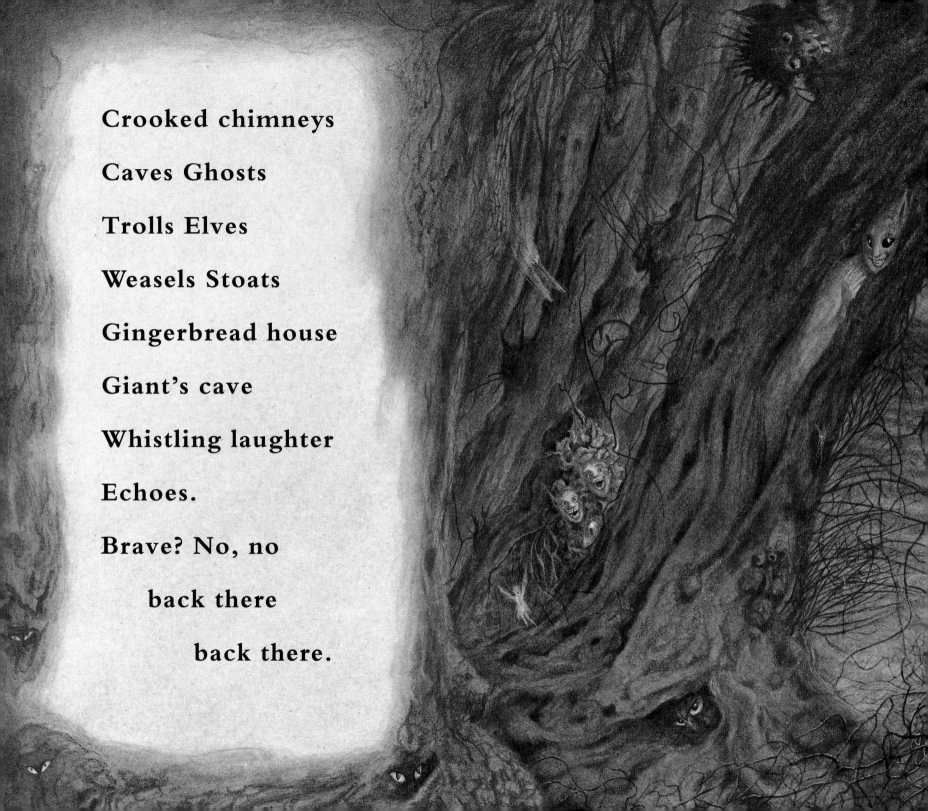

Crooked chimneys

Caves Ghosts

Trolls Elves

Weasels Stoats

Gingerbread house

Giant's cave

Whistling laughter

Echoes.

Brave? No, no

back there

back there.

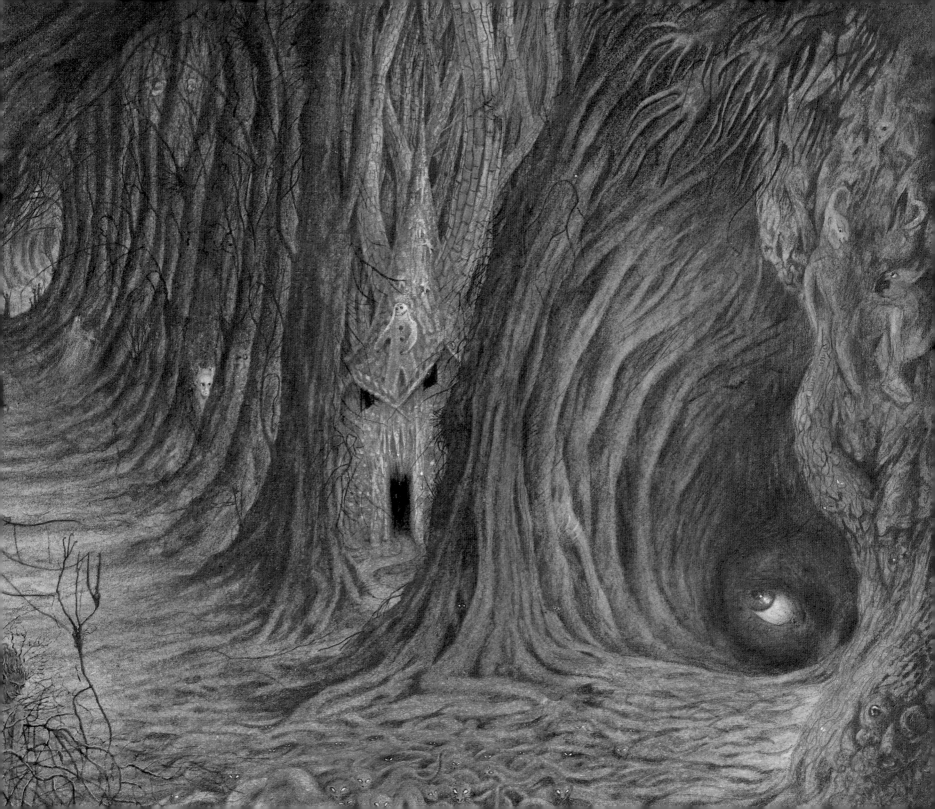

Oh, *where?*

Oh, there.

Kitchen's warm.

Smells of spice.

Curtains drawn.

Fire bright.

Night.

But *what's* out there?